SEARCHING FOR THE ACORN

BY DEBORAH LATZKE

DEDICATED TO EACH COURAGEOUS READER IN SEARCH
OF THE TRUTH THAT LIES WITHIN.

WITH HEARTFELT GRATITUDE TO EACH INDIVIDUAL WHOSE VALUABLE TIME AND
ENERGY HELPED SHAPE THE STORY FROM CONCEPT TO COMPLETION.

SPECIAL THANKS TO . . .
PAM SCHOFFNER WHOSE WISE, GENTLE GUIDANCE THROUGHOUT THE EDITING PROCESS ADDED
CLARITY NOT ONLY TO THE STORY, BUT ALSO TO MY OWN JOURNEY AS A WRITER.

PEGGY LAURITSEN DESIGN GROUP FOR ONCE AGAIN, CREATING AN INSPIRED & BEAUTIFUL BOOK DESIGN.

IDEAL PRINTERS, INC. FOR THEIR QUALITY WORKMANSHIP AND SUPPORTIVE SPIRIT.

"WHAT LIES BEHIND US,
AND WHAT LIES BEFORE US
ARE TINY MATTERS
COMPARED TO WHAT
LIES WITHIN US."

RALPH WALDO EMERSON

Yewmi's Search

Yewmi sat at the edge of the enchanted forest and gazed at the canopy of starlight above her. She anxiously searched the night sky until she found the brightest star of all and silently wished for an answer to calm the turbulence she felt inside. So many questions about the meaning and purpose of her life; so few answers for living with boundless love and joy. Suddenly a shooting star pulled Yewmi's attention from her self-doubts. As she watched the brilliant spark leave a trail of star dust in its wake, Yewmi sensed the light was somehow a clue that the answers she sought were near.

Whether or not Yewmi wanted to admit it, she had reached a crossroads. Did she want to take the path that would lead to more of the same or travel the path to create something different? Though the question appeared to be a simple one, the answer was not easy. One choice would lead her to the known, the familiar, and the way it's always been. It was a choice that offered the illusion of security, of predictable outcomes and known consequences. This safe path was tempting, but Yewmi intuitively understood it was a choice that would keep life's most precious secrets locked away. The path to creating something different would lead her into the unknown, the unfamiliar, and the uncharted territory of change. It was a choice that came without predictable outcomes and required taking risks. To Yewmi, it represented passage through a dark and forbidding tunnel of unnamed fears. It was a choice she had avoided her entire life.

Was unlocking the secrets worth facing her fears? The instant the question formed in her mind, Yewmi began to sense an ominous, almost palpable presence. Her heart began pounding out of control. The air surrounding her became thick and putrid, making it difficult to breathe. Yewmi squeezed her eyes shut and desperately wished she could magically return to the safety of her village before panic completely consumed her. Alas, it was too late. When she opened her eyes, the heinous, predatory creature of fear had stepped from the dark shadows and stood before her. Frightened to the very core of her being, Yewmi scrambled to her feet and ran as fast as she could away from the fear and into the enchanted forest.

Yewmi was deep into the woods before she dared to look back. The fear was nowhere in sight, but she could still feel its suffocating presence. Alarmed, Yewmi questioned her instinctive flight into the forest. Why hadn't she run back to the village instead? She had no idea where she was or how to get home. In an effort to get her bearings — and to make certain that the fear was not lurking behind one of the nearby trees — Yewmi began slowly turning in a circle. As she turned, a campfire flickering in the distance came into view. Hoping to find help, Yewmi hurried toward the light.

THE ANCIENT WISE ONE AND THE COUNCIL OF WISDOM

As Yewmi drew closer to the campfire, she entered a clearing in the dense forest. The opening was defined by a circle of towering oak trees with branches that twinkled with light as though filled with thousands of fireflies. At the center of the circle, sitting before the fire, was the ancient Wise One, the last remaining member of the legendary Council of Wisdom. Yewmi rubbed her eyes in disbelief, but they had not deceived her. According to the legend, the Council members had provided daily guidance to many generations who lived near the enchanted forest. Those who sought their counsel returned speaking of magic and miracles. Yewmi timidly approached the old sage, bowed in reverence and was beckoned to sit near the fire.

As Yewmi sat down, she searched the Wise One's face for a flicker of recognition — some sign that her deepest feelings and fears were somehow understood by the powerful sage. Seeing nothing but a warm smile reflecting back at her, Yewmi paused to gather her thoughts before sharing them. "I am in need of your counsel, Wise One. Tonight, I saw my fear. Instead of standing my ground and facing it, I ran away. I'm not ready yet. I'm not sure I'll ever be ready."

The Wise One allowed silence to fill the space between them. After several minutes, the ancient counselor spoke from the heart. "Dear Yewmi, you are ready or you would not have found your way here to this moment in time. Your truth waits just beyond your fear. To you, it appears you were running away from the fear. To me, it appears you were running toward the truth. In recognizing your fear, you have already traveled further than some ever do. Fear comes in many disguises and wears many masks, but in the end, it is always the same. It is an illusion we create — a dark shadow where love and light have been denied access. Fear is where we hide from our true nature and purpose. It can exist only when we do not know and trust who we truly are. It is fear that keeps the most precious secrets of life locked away. Know this, Yewmi, you are ready to step from the shadow and into the light or you would not be here."

Yewmi turned her gaze from the Wise One, looked into the darkness beyond the firelight and shook her head. "I want to believe you. But, I don't feel ready. I only feel the fear." The Wise One smiled, took Yewmi's hand and said, "Let me tell you the story of the first sacred journey."

The First Sacred Journey

"It was a time long, long ago, before the journey of creating a life filled with love and joy became a matter of choice. A group of men, women and children called the Acorn People lived here in the enchanted forest. Having been taught and nurtured by the Council of Wisdom, each member of the Acorn Community knew the secret to living a joyful life. They knew the true meaning of loving, honoring and respecting everyone and everything. They especially knew the importance of trusting the power of that love.

"Several generations of Acorn People flourished, dwelling together in harmony of purpose and living their entire lives in the magical safety of the enchanted forest. Then, hundreds of years before you were born, the Council of Wisdom sent notice to each member of the Acorn Community. It was time to venture into the world beyond the enchanted forest and share their secret. And so it was, Yewmi, that the village where you now live was founded.

"Life beyond the magical forest provided new challenges for the Acorn People. Within a few short decades, the Acorn People began to forget their true nature and purpose. They began to take on the human qualities of fear, doubt and worry. The Council of Wisdom convened and devised a plan to help the Acorn People remember their powerful secret before it became lost forever.

"Seven members of the Acorn Community were summoned by the Council of Wisdom. Each was presented with a single, sacred acorn from the enchanted forest and instructed to embark on a journey. The purpose of the journey was to search out a place where the acorn could be planted and nurtured, thus allowing its promise to unfold and flourish.

"Although it was not revealed to them, the seven were chosen on the basis of their fears. The Council of Wisdom understood that the challenges of such a journey would intensify their fears, but also would provide each with the opportunity to relinquish fear's powerful hold and choose love in its place.

"All seven were fully capable of succeeding at the task they had been given. When they met the challenge, the secrets of their true nature and purpose would, once again, be revealed. Hope for humanity would, once again, be restored."

As Yewmi listened, she realized she was not alone in her fear. Others had felt it, too. Maybe there was hope after all. She settled in as the ancient Wise One revealed the seven stories of the first sacred journey.

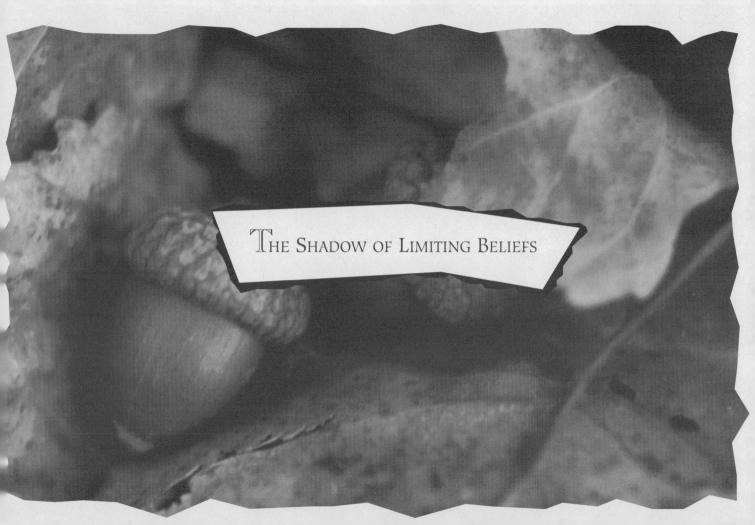

The Shadow of Limiting Beliefs

Hannah resented being chosen for the first sacred journey, a senseless tour of the countryside in search of a place to plant a silly acorn. This was one more burden, yet another hardship, for her to bear. Hannah had been orphaned at the age of nine and taken in by her widowed aunt. Though well-meaning, Hannah's aunt was a rather cold-hearted woman who lived a lonely life of bitterness and blame. She felt obligated to take Hannah in, but had little to offer her beyond shelter, food and clothing. In time, Hannah began to forget the life she had lived before and what it felt like to be loved and adored. Sadly, with the passing of each year, she grew to resemble her aunt more and more. By the time she was chosen for the journey, Hannah had come to believe she was a powerless victim of fate; convinced that life — especially her life — was meant to be difficult. Nevertheless, she was given a single, sacred acorn and sent on her way.

Because she had been focused on the adversities of her life, Hannah found herself poorly prepared for the day-to-day demands of the journey. She had neglected to pack sturdy walking shoes and warm, protective clothing. By the end of the first day, her feet were blistered and terribly sore. By the end of the first week, she was exhausted from tending the fire throughout the night to keep herself warm. Hannah felt the task she had been given was cruel and pointless. As her journey progressed, thoughts of loneliness, misery and gloom were Hannah's constant companions.

Many she met along the way offered her comfort and assured her that her journey did, indeed, have a grand purpose. She did not, could not, hear them. She could only feel the misfortune of her predicament and wonder angrily how she was supposed to know where to plant the acorn she had grown to despise. The Council had told her what to do, but had failed to tell her where, when or how to carry out the task. If it was such an important job they should not have chosen her to do it! Hannah was convinced the task was beyond her. She could see no solution and no end in sight to her dismal situation. Each step she took seemed to fuel her resentment, and there had been many, many steps.

Hannah had been traveling for several months and still had no idea where to plant the acorn. One evening, as dusk began to blanket the world, she sat down in a state of exhaustion under the shelter of a tall oak tree. Too tired to prepare her evening meal, Hannah wrapped herself in a tattered blanket, leaned against the trunk of the tree and allowed it to support the weight of her weary body. The thought of another day of aimless wandering was too much for her to bear. Before she drifted off to sleep, Hannah did something she had never done before in her entire life. She hoped for a solution and asked for help to find it. Her last thoughts before succumbing to slumber were, "Please help me. I know there's an answer."

That night, Hannah dreamed a dream like never before. In it, she was walking through a heavy, dense fog when suddenly she stepped out of the mist and into a familiar meadow filled with dazzling sunlight. As she basked in the radiant energy surrounding her, Hannah began to remember what love felt like. The more she focused on the love, the more powerful and full of possibilities she felt. Even as she slept, the dream brought her great comfort and joy. For the first time in months, she slept peacefully and awoke with a smile on her face. Hannah knew! Less than a mile from her home was a meadow like the one in the dream. She had passed through it many times, but had not realized its extraordinary beauty until now. It would be a wonderful place to plant the acorn!

A change had taken place within Hannah that could not be explained merely by the elation of knowing how to complete her task. She had come to an important realization about herself. She had believed from the beginning that her journey would be difficult and that, indeed, is what she had experienced. In the midst of those limiting thoughts, she had missed the beauty of the people and places that had surrounded her each day.

She also had overlooked the simple solution to the task and created a completely unnecessary hardship. Hannah packed her blanket, gathered a plentiful supply of wild berries to satisfy her hunger, and began her return journey. As she walked the road toward home, she thought about the dream and knew it was a powerful message to focus on possibilities, not limitations — on the positive, not the negative — on the solutions, not the problems. The power to choose was hers and hers alone. From that moment on, Hannah knew she would choose wisely and always with love.

The Shadow of Diminished Joy

David was pleased to be chosen for the sacred journey. He knew immediately where he would plant the acorn. When he was very young, David's grandmother had shared her memories of the extraordinary village she lived in as a child. She always meant to return for a visit, but life had a way of distracting her from so many things she intended to do. She died without fulfilling her desire. Traveling to his grandmother's village and planting the acorn there would be David's gift to her memory. He packed and left that very day.

It was a two-week journey, and David enjoyed every step. He made many friends along the way; stopping to listen to the life stories of those he met, sharing the feast his wife had packed, helping to mend a fence. Wherever David went, good things seemed to happen. He left everyone and everything he came into contact with somehow better, and he liked that. He liked that very much. It made him feel good inside to be helpful and to make a contribution. His grandmother had often spoken to him about the art of giving, and David relished the thought that he had mastered the art.

At last, David arrived at the village his grandmother so fondly remembered. Word of his identity and the nature of his visit spread quickly. David was welcomed joyously and warmly embraced as an honorary member of the community. The village elders met with David, and the site for the planting was chosen. The acorn would be planted in the village square the following day.

Several villagers approached David vying for the privilege of providing him with food and lodging for the night. His reply to each was the same, "Your kind gesture is appreciated but I prefer to sleep under the stars and have plenty of provisions for an evening meal."

An elderly woman introduced herself as a friend of his grandmother's. "I have a blanket and a few sticks of firewood that will help keep you warm in the chilly night air. I would be honored if you would accept them as my gift." David expressed his gratitude to the frail old woman but gently informed her that he had everything he needed.

A group of excited elders approached next with their plans for the planting ceremony, which would be followed by a grand celebration. Once again, David declined. "Thank you, but I really would like to take care of the details myself."

The village elders conferred briefly and approached David as he began unpacking. The mayor stepped forward, his eyes filled with sadness. "I'm sorry, David. We cannot accept your gift."

David looked at him with astonishment. Surely there had been some sort of misunderstanding. He explained to the elders that the gift was sacred and that it was given freely, at no expense to the villagers. He assured them that he expected nothing in return other than allowing the acorn to grow and become a magnificent oak tree.

The elders lowered their eyes as David spoke. When he finished, the mayor shook his head slowly. "It is because the gift is sacred that we cannot accept it from you — not in the manner in which you have offered it. We assumed your grandmother had shared with you our belief about the Cycle of Joy and passed it on to you as her legacy. It is a legacy each of us in this village promises to share."

David interrupted, "If you mean the lesson of giving to others, she did talk about it a great deal as I was growing up. I know about giving. I've dedicated my life to it. Don't you understand? That's why I'm here."

The mayor's reply was adamant. "No, David. It is you who does not understand. I think, perhaps, your grandmother did speak to you about the Cycle of Joy, but you heard only what you wanted to hear. You chose to place great value in giving to others as a means of affirming your own worth and importance. Consequently, you learned to place very little value in the act of receiving."

David felt confused. "Is it so wrong to feel good about bringing pleasure to others?"

"It is not a question of right or wrong. It is a question of diminished joy. A true gift is given from a place of pure joy — without conditions and without thought of what is to be gained. The cycle is completed when the gift is received from a place of pure joy — without hesitation and without thought of indebtedness.

The cycle is about giving and receiving from that place of joy. In this respect, you have much yet to learn. We must ask you to continue on your journey and send you on your way with one wish . . . that you will, one day soon, know the joy of allowing the cycle to be complete."

David reluctantly packed and left the village that night. As he walked along the dark road, David thought about the mayor's words. It was true. He gave, more often than not, because it made him feel appreciated and important. Receiving made him feel uncomfortable. It seemed to diminish his value and create a sense of obligation and debt. Neither his giving nor his hesitant, limited receiving came from a place of pure joy. He walked all night, pondering how he could experience the Cycle of Joy.

Just as the sun began to rise over the horizon, the solution to his dilemma became clear! David hurried home, went directly to the garden behind his cottage, and planted the sacred acorn where he would see it grow every day. As he laid the sacred seed in the warm, nurturing soil, David felt a tremendous surge of joy! The cycle of giving and receiving was complete. He understood, at last, that together they make an act of love. Where better to begin than with oneself!

The Shadow of Doing

Ariel felt honored to have been chosen for the sacred journey. As a very busy woman with a great many responsibilities, Ariel always recognized an important task and she added the journey to her long list of things to be done. Her first priority, however, was her family's annual acorn harvest. As the oldest child in her family, Ariel had inherited the grove of oak trees that supplied the entire village with acorns. She painstakingly tended to the trees and nurtured them daily to ensure a plentiful harvest each year. In addition to being the diligent caretaker of the oak grove, Ariel was a loving and attentive wife, mother and grandmother. Her daily life was filled with people and things to care for — and had been for as long as she could remember. Everyone was counting on her. The sacred journey would have to wait.

Ariel's list of duties after the harvest included sorting, storing and planting the acorns to guarantee there would always be a supply on hand for future generations. When these tasks were completed, it would be time to clean and repair the equipment, take inventory, order supplies for the coming spring and mend the baskets used to gather the acorns. The little spare time she did have was devoted to her loved ones and the endless responsibilities of being a family matriarch.

Wistful thoughts of the sacred journey came and went frequently without Ariel taking any action on them. Everything else on her list of things to do seemed to take priority. There just didn't seem to be enough time to get everything done. The seasons passed filled with the responsibilities of caring for the oak grove and her family. Each year she vowed she would find time for herself and her sacred journey. A decade later, Ariel still had not kept her promise.

One beautiful September day, Ariel was busy working in the oak grove, making last-minute preparations for the acorn harvest. It was her favorite time of year. The autumn air was crisp and cool. The sky was a deep azure blue, and the leaves of her beloved trees had begun to turn to shades of magenta and crimson. Although she had many tasks yet to complete, Ariel paused, closed her eyes, inhaled deeply and breathed in the splendor of the afternoon. For a few precious moments she allowed herself to be fully present to the serenity of her surroundings. As an oak leaf slowly floated down from the branch overhead and landed on her shoulder, Ariel began to feel a deep sense of peace and contentment. She smiled as she opened her eyes, removed the leaf, and carefully tucked it into the pocket of her skirt.

When she looked up, she noticed her youngest granddaughter sitting beneath one of the majestic oak trees and looking somewhat forlorn. Ariel approached her and, without a word, sat down beside her, gently took her hand and held it lovingly in her own. After a few moments of silence, Ariel said, "Something seems to be bothering you. Would you like to talk about it?"

"Oh Grandma, I want to go on an adventure with my friends, but the acorn harvest is the busiest time of year. I know I should stay here and help like everyone else in the family, but I really, really want to go. If I stay and help with the harvest, I'll miss the fun of the adventure. If I go, I'll feel guilty the whole time and ruin the fun. I don't know what to do."

As Ariel considered her granddaughter's dilemma, she remembered the oak leaf and responded from a wise place deep in her heart that had been silent for many years. "It's important to take responsibility for your own life . . . to make choices that are right for you and that bring joy to you. That doesn't make you selfish or irresponsible. It means you value yourself and pay attention to your dreams and desires." As Ariel spoke, she removed the leaf from her pocket and looked at the gentle reminder. "Getting up in the morning, staying busy, working hard and doing things for others is not what makes us valuable." She tenderly caressed her granddaughter's cheek and continued, "I'm sorry if my words and actions over the years may have taught you to believe that our value comes from what we do. I know now that it comes from appreciating and enjoying who we are at this moment in time. If I had one wish, it would be that I had spent less time doing and more time being. Maybe you can learn from my mistakes. It's not too late for you."

After her granddaughter had gone back to the village, Ariel remained behind. She sat beneath the tree for a long time as leaves silently fell around her. The words of wisdom that had been buried deep within echoed over and over in her mind. By the time dusk had settled in, Ariel had reached a momentous decision. She stood up and walked home, feeling renewal and resolve with every step.

Ariel rose before dawn the next morning. She packed a picnic, placed the sacred acorn next to the oak leaf in her pocket, and quietly closed the door behind her. She walked the short distance to her granddaughter's home and placed the leaf on the doorstep with this note:

For my beloved granddaughter . . .
Sometimes we get so busy we forget what's really important.
Thank you for helping me remember . . . it's never too late!
With love and gratitude,
Grandma

Keeping the promise she had made more than a decade before, Ariel left on her journey to plant the sacred acorn. The path she followed was one she had walked a thousand times before. But, on this day, she noticed and appreciated something new with every step she took. Ariel's journey led her to the heart of the oak grove. Having reached her destination, she spread the blanket she had brought on the ground and sat down to watch the sunrise. She savored each moment as the night sky slowly surrendered to a breathtaking array of vibrant colors. Afterwards she enjoyed her picnic breakfast and watched the squirrels as they scurried to and fro in search of acorns. The frantic pace of their activity reminded Ariel of the woman she used to be. She smiled and called out to the busy little creatures, "Slow down! It's a glorious day!" On that note, she stood up, retrieved the sacred acorn from her pocket and planted it. Watching it grow would be an ever-present reminder: to shift her focus from the next task at hand to the precious moment at hand; to enjoy life; to be still and appreciate quiet solitude; and, to reflect on the changes she would make to enhance the peace and contentment she desired and deserved. Ariel had learned, at last, to cherish the experience of being.

When she returned from the oak grove, Ariel posted a notice in the village square inviting everyone to the first annual Acorn Harvest Festival. Delighted by the opportunity to help Ariel and her family, the entire community assembled at the grove. They brought baskets for gathering acorns and a bountiful feast for the celebration. Ariel's brother played his fiddle and filled the autumn air with festive music. The acorns soon were gathered but the light-hearted camaraderie continued until dusk. Ariel summoned everyone together as the sun began to set and thanked them for making the day so enjoyable. As the villagers began to head for home, Ariel watched a single leaf slowly drift to the ground and whispered, "Thank you."

THE SHADOW OF THE COMFORT ZONE

Aurora felt terrified when she heard she was chosen for the sacred journey. She had spent her entire life in the village. The journey would require her to leave the safe familiarity of her comfortable home and courageously travel into the world beyond. How would she, who knew nothing of life beyond the village walls, know where to go or what to do? The thought of the unknown made her tremble. Aurora found no consolation in disclosing her fears to her friends and family. Each had told her the only way to conquer her fear of the unknown would be to venture into it. Everyone seemed to think it would be a wonderful opportunity. Aurora thought it was the worst thing that could have happened to her.

But seeing no way to decline, Aurora left on her journey early the next morning. Her knees felt weak and her heart was nearly pounding out of her chest when she stepped through the village gates. She wanted to turn back, but her family and friends had already closed the gates and were standing on the opposite side of the wall cheering, waving and wishing her good luck. Aurora walked slowly down the road until the village was just out of sight and then sat down. She thought for a very long time about what to do since she couldn't return without finding a place to plant the acorn. Aurora finally decided she would travel each day as far as she could see and, having reached that point off in the distance, she would travel another one hundred steps for good measure. Yes, that felt reasonably safe, she thought. Even she might be able to do that. Don't think about what lies ahead, she told herself. Just focus on the next step. Put one foot in front of the other and take the step.

And so Aurora's journey began. She spent most of the first day looking down at her feet, concentrating on making them move. Much to her surprise, she reached the lone pine tree she had seen on the horizon that morning and chosen as her stopping point. Aurora took the last one hundred steps and set up camp. She cooked a simple meal over the campfire and settled in for the night.

With the goals and tasks for the day completed, there was nothing to focus her thoughts on, and once again Aurora's fears loomed before her. She had never spent a night alone in the wilderness, and a thousand worrisome "what if's" began to thunder through her mind. In a state of terror, she pulled the blanket up over her head and wept until she fell into a troubled sleep.

Aurora traveled for several days, stretching the limits of her comfort zone each day and sleeping with the blanket over her head each night. During the middle of the seventh night, the sound of a hooting owl awoke Aurora. The blanket had fallen from her face and she opened her eyes to the breathtaking sight of the Aurora Borealis dancing across the sky. It was the most beautiful spectacle she had ever seen. Aurora remembered being told she had been born on just such a night and that was how she had acquired her name. Lying snug and warm under the blanket, Aurora allowed herself to become enchanted by the lights, and they began to speak to her in a comforting voice. Over and over they repeated the same phrase. "You are safe. You are safe. You are safe."

Aurora realized that her fears and worries about her journey had been a waste of precious time and energy. She had been safe each step of the way. It was true, she had gotten a few bumps and bruises when she stumbled and fell down a ravine. She had strayed off the path and been lost on several occasions. She had even encountered a scary creature or two along the way. But the fact remained she was safe and sound looking up at the dazzling light display. Aurora realized she would have missed the beauty of this night had she not faced her fears and ventured into the unknown. She watched the magical lights dance across the night sky until darkness began to give way to the dawn of a new day. Trusting that her safety came from a powerful place within, she surrendered to a serene slumber.

The next morning Aurora planted her acorn on the spot where she had slept. As she laid the sacred seed into the safekeeping of the soil, she made a silent promise to herself: whenever she felt certain that she was stretched to the limits of her courage and ability, she would stretch again. She would dare to risk that awesome leap of faith.

Aurora decided to continue on her journey, curious to see what was just beyond the next horizon. She was delighted and amazed to find sights and sounds and smells beyond her wildest imagination. After several months of travel, Aurora found herself standing on a pristine beach, looking out over a vast expanse of sapphire blue water. Before she turned to begin her trip home, she gazed longingly at the distant horizon and silently vowed her next adventure would take her across this great body of water to the wonderful, magical "what if" that waited for her on the distant shore.

The Shadow of Needing Validation

Michael saw his selection for the sacred journey as a wonderful opportunity. He was the youngest child in his family and had walked in the shadow of his siblings for as long as he could remember. This would be his chance to shine, to show everyone that he, too, was capable of great things. If he could earn the approval and admiration of the Council of Wisdom, he was sure to receive the accolades and recognition of his family and friends. Michael filled a large burlap sack with extra acorns to plant. That way, he would not only meet, but exceed, everyone's expectations. Within an hour of being chosen by the Council, Michael had departed on his journey.

A few miles from the village, Michael followed a path into a forest and hurriedly planted the sacred acorn. He was anxious to continue on his journey and to plant as many acorns as he could while daylight remained. Each time he planted one of the acorns,

Michael made an entry in his journal as evidence of his extraordinary endeavors to show the Council. When he had planted all his acorns, he began to gather more. Each day of his journey was the same. From sunup until sundown he gathered and planted acorns. If he ran out of daylight before finishing his allotted plantings for that day, he worked into the night, carrying a torch so he could see in the darkness.

It wasn't long before Michael and his acorns began to gain attention. People really seemed to like the idea of having their own acorns, not to plant as Michael did, but just to polish and display in baskets. Seeing the possibility for a new opportunity to enhance his achievements, he decided he had planted plenty of acorns and would begin selling them instead. He would make money — perhaps a great deal of money! He would donate a generous portion of his profits to the village and earn even more approval and recognition.

The demand for acorns continued to grow, making it difficult for Michael to keep a ready supply on hand. It took time to gather so many acorns and time was money. One day, Michael met a man adept at wood carving and he was suddenly inspired. He hired the man to carve decorative wooden acorns for people to display. He soon hired several more carvers and before he knew it, the profits from selling the wooden acorns had made him a very wealthy man. Michael was ready at last to return to his village.

As Michael got closer to home, he began to remember the sacred purpose of his journey. The more he thought about it, the more confused he became. He had exceeded everyone's expectations. He had planted hundreds of acorns and sold thousands more. He was wealthy. No one could possibly question his success. Then, why didn't he feel more joyful about what he had accomplished on his journey?

The night before his return, Michael camped in the forest where he had planted the sacred acorn. He felt a surge of joy when he saw that the seed he had planted so long ago had taken root. A tiny, tender shoot had emerged from the nurturing soil. He envisioned the fragile, newborn tree growing for one hundred years or more to become a magnificent oak. It didn't matter that very few people, if any at all, would bear witness to its beauty or know that he was the one who gave it life. He would know. Suddenly, Michael realized that the tiny tree had given him the answer to why he had felt so little pleasure on his journey. Every choice he had made and every action he had taken had been based on his desire to earn the approval of others. The sacred acorn had taught him that one's value is not something that can be given to you or taken away from you. It comes from inside. And, like the acorn, its promise will unfold and flourish of its own accord if it is nurtured from within.

Michael returned home the next day. He never spoke of his achievements and he anonymously donated his acorn profits to those in need. Each year, on the anniversary of the sacred planting, he took his children and then his grandchildren and great grandchildren to see the oak and celebrate its growth. And, each year as they sat beneath the tree, he told them the story of a man who had traveled great distances to discover that what he had been searching for could only be found within himself.

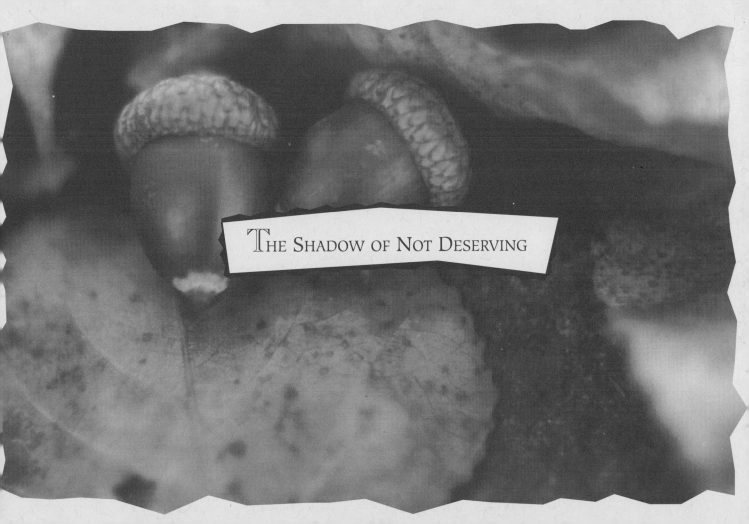

THE SHADOW OF NOT DESERVING

Grace felt certain there must have been a mistake when she heard that she had been chosen for the sacred journey. She did not feel important enough to justify such an honor. In her eyes, Grace had led a small and insignificant life. She lived a quiet and solitary existence in a disheveled thatch-roofed cottage near the edge of the village. Selling firewood in the market square provided her with income for only the most meager necessities. Grace had come to believe that what you see is what you get and what you get is what you deserve. Obviously, she didn't deserve much. If she did, she would have more: more comforts, more fun and more people who loved and cared about her. She often fantasized about a better, easier life, but nothing ever changed. Long ago, Grace had taught herself to accept what seemed to be her fate and tried hard not to envy others for their good fortune.

After checking with the Council to make sure they had, indeed, chosen her, Grace packed a few of her belongings with the sacred acorn in a knapsack and departed on her journey. She found several places she thought might be good locations to plant the acorn, but each time, she hesitated, not trusting herself to make such an important decision. Grace continued on her search until one day when the clouds burst open in a downpour and rain forced her to seek shelter in a nearby barn. When the storm passed, she looked out and saw a magnificent rainbow spread across the entire horizon. As Grace stared at the dazzling arc of color, she was amazed to hear a gentle voice coming from somewhere inside her. It said, "Plant the acorn at the site of the rainbow."

Grace timidly walked up the lane toward the house near the barn and hoped the owner would grant her permission to plant the acorn. When she knocked on the door, an elderly woman appeared and invited her into her home. From the moment Grace stepped inside and explained her request, she was treated like a queen. The stranger's kindness was beyond anything she had ever experienced before. To refresh Grace from her travels, she was offered a warm bath, given a clean gown to wear and invited to share a sumptuous meal with her hostess.

After they dined, the old woman served tea and apple cobbler beside the fire. When she was certain Grace was comfortable, she sat down and said, "You haven't told me much about yourself."

Grace shrugged her shoulders. "There's not much to tell. My life really hasn't amounted to much."

The old woman smiled. "Oh, I doubt that very much. Please, start at the beginning."

And so Grace talked and the woman listened. When Grace finished, her companion's face was beaming. "You're a very determined, resourceful, strong young woman! I can understand why the Council chose you for such an important task."

Grace looked into the twinkling eyes of her benevolent hostess. She had never thought of herself that way. "When you say it, I almost believe it."

"I'm only speaking the truth. If you listen carefully, you will hear a voice that comes from inside of you telling you the same thing."

Grace was invited to stay for the night. Later, as she climbed into bed, she wondered if the voice the old woman had spoken of was the one that had told her where to plant the acorn. Nestled in the comfort of fine linen and soft down, Grace listened for the voice until she drifted off to sleep.

Early the next morning, the two women walked to the meadow where Grace had seen the rainbow. Together they dug a small hole and as Grace carefully laid the seed in the welcoming soil, the elderly woman thanked her for choosing her land upon which to plant the acorn. Grace looked at the woman in disbelief. "I'm the one who should be thanking you! Not just for a place to plant the acorn, but for the extraordinary evening. I've never experienced such care and kindness in my entire life. You went to too much bother just to show your gratitude for the acorn."

"Oh, my dear," the elderly woman explained, "what I did was not because of the acorn. It was because of you! I treated you the way you deserve to be treated . . . like the precious being that you are. I was raised to believe that each of us, as the spark of light and love that we are, deserves the best . . . from ourselves, from each other and from life. We come into this world that way and we leave that way, too. But what we experience in-between is up to us. My dear Grace, you have tremendous value and deserve good even beyond what you can imagine." As the wise old woman finished speaking, Grace's beautiful brown eyes glistened with tears. The words had touched her deeply. Grace knew she had been given a great gift . . . the gift of truth.

After she warmly embraced her companion, Grace headed for home. What Grace believed to be true about herself and about her life changed from that day on. Every day during the long trip home, she listened for and heard the voice from deep within. She began to think of it as her truest friend. One day the voice asked her, "What do you really want to do with your life?"

Without a moment's hesitation, Grace replied, "I want to weave beautiful baskets that bring pleasure to others by making their daily chores a bit easier and more enjoyable." She couldn't wait to arrive home and begin her new venture.

In the weeks that followed, Grace's little cottage hummed with activity. The baskets she lovingly made became one of the most popular items in the village market. Several customers became her good friends. Grace often invited them to sit with her in the garden she had planted after returning from her journey. And each morning of her life, Grace went to the garden, sat on a beautiful wooden bench that she had made and listened for her inner voice.

THE SHADOW OF PERFECTION

Marcus was thrilled to be chosen for the sacred journey. He immediately sat down and made a list of things to do before his departure. The first task was research. Taking careful notes, he read every book he could get his hands on pertaining to the oak tree and its preferred habitat. Then he gathered his equipment: a soil-testing kit, divining rod, maps, his research notes, and, of course, the sacred acorn. Amply prepared and bearing a large backpack of supplies, Marcus departed with a feeling of euphoria. He would find the perfect place to plant the acorn — with the perfect climate and soil conditions. Marcus was determined that his acorn would grow to be the biggest and the best oak tree in all the land.

Marcus stopped to check the soil conditions several times a day. Each time, the spot he had selected fell short in one or more of the variables he determined necessary to be perfect. Several weeks after his departure, a young man who bore a remarkable resemblance to Marcus approached him and offered this advice: "Listen to your heart. It has something important to tell you." The young man continued on his path before Marcus could question the cryptic message.

The search went on for several more years. Marcus became driven by his unrelenting need to settle for nothing less than perfection. Each day ended in frustration but as the sun rose the following morning, Marcus was renewed with the hope that he would find exactly what he was looking for that day.

One afternoon, he stopped to examine the soil conditions. It had been a spectacularly beautiful day with crystal blue skies and a warm, gentle breeze. But totally absorbed in his analytical procedures since early morning, Marcus had barely noticed. As he bent over his most recent soil sample, a middle-aged man walked up and observed him in silence for several minutes. Then the man spoke. "What you seek cannot be found in the soil."

"You're right," Marcus replied. "At least not in this soil. It's too dry. Maybe it's better down the road a bit." The stranger walked away slowly with a sad expression.

Many years of searching passed. Marcus had become an old man. One day, as he hobbled along the road, an elderly man who looked vaguely familiar approached. The stranger leaned on his walking stick, looked deeply into Marcus' eyes and said, "I see you are still on your quest to find perfection. What you seek is where you stand." Marcus looked at the soil beneath his feet and gathered a fistful of the black dirt. He shook his head and let the soil slowly slip through his fingers. When Marcus looked up, the old man had vanished.

Many years later, a traveler stopped to rest for the night near the Acorn Community. She told the story of a man who had been on a life-long quest. He died in a faraway land clutching an acorn to his breast. Those who found the man buried him with the acorn still in his hand, resting over his heart. A majestic oak tree grows there on that very spot today . . . a powerful testament revealing that Marcus had, indeed, succeeded in finding the perfect place to plant the sacred seed of love.

Making Wise and Loving Choices

Having finished the story, the Wise One looked intently at Yewmi. "Dear one, I do understand when you speak of your fear. You see, I was one of the seven chosen for that first sacred journey. We each were chosen because we harbored fears deep inside. The sacred journey provided us with the opportunity to face and overcome those fears. Sharing the story with you is my way of reassuring you that you are not alone and offering you hope.

"It is a wise and courageous act to face your fear. It is only in that moment of truth that one realizes the choice that exists for each of us: to base our lives on love or on fear . . . to step toward the light of our true nature or into the shadows of self-imposed limitations. When we recognize that the choice is indeed ours to make, we begin to realize that fear is only an illusion.

"We are born beings of light and love. We die beings of light and love. The journey between birth and death is filled with an infinite array of opportunities to discover the power of the love that is our birthright. It is a love that transcends all fears, doubts and limitations. It allows us to step out of the shadow of believing we are not worthy of such a love and into the light of knowing we *are* the love. The only unknown is which we will choose.

"Dear Yewmi, choose wisely and with love . . . and remember to be gentle with yourself. The acorn is who you really are and the sacred journey is your life. There is only one guarantee on the journey. The acorn will always be there for you, waiting patiently to be discovered."

All that remained of the campfire were a few glowing embers. The ancient Wise One slowly rose, bowed to Yewmi and said, "The light within me salutes the light within you." Yewmi watched as the Wise One vanished before her eyes . . . but not before placing a single, sacred acorn in the palm of her hand.

THE BEGINNING . . . .

Books by Deborah Latzke

When the Last Acorn is Found

Searching for the Acorn